The Christmas Nisse

story

Written by

Patrick Nielsen

decorated by
Epilogue Books
Robyn Wilson-Owen

First Printing: 2017

ISBN 978-1-78808-824-4

Epilogue Books
Cambridge, UK

Dedication

To Rachel and Freya for all their encouragement, enthusiasm and boundless love and affection for Anna-Lise.

To my parents, sister and family for all of their help and support, and all those grown-ups and children who have given helpful suggestions along the way.

To all the children (and adults!) in my classes who have listened to the story over the years and shared their ideas to help it evolve.

To Robyn for illustrating the book with her wonderful pictures and helping to bring the words to life.

And last, but certainly not least, to Anna-Lise, the nisse who comes to our house with treats every December who inspired the story.

Before You Read

This book is an advent calendar book, so it is intended to be read, preferably at bedtime, one chapter a day during December in the lead-up to Christmas.

This is why the chapters have dates, showing which day each one is meant to be read on. You can choose to read it however you want, but the experience is best if you do it like this.

The book is inspired by my Scandinavian roots, and so there are a few Nordic words and names which readers might not immediately know how to pronounce.

Pronunciation guide:

Nisse – [ˈnɪsə], i.e. **Ni** as in 'ni**bble**'; **e** as in **ur** in 'surprise'

Anna-Lise - [ˈanaˈliːsə], i.e. **Lis** as in '**lease**', and **e** as in the **e** in 'Nisse'

Hygge - [ˈhygə], i.e. **y** as in **u** in French 'd**u**'; **gg** as in 'bi**gg**er', and **e** (again) as the **e** in 'Nisse'

Erna - [ˈɛəna], i.e. **Er** as **ere** in 'th**ere**'; **na** as in the end of 'bana**na**'

Santa Lucia - [ˈsantaluˈsiːa], i.e. **Lu** with short vowel as in '**Lu**cy'; **ci** as in '**see**', and the last **a** as in 'vi**a**'

Note: In phonetic writing the symbol ' marks stress on the next syllable.

Contents

Prologue

Astrid Andersen peeked out of her window, hoping to catch a glimpse of something special. December had arrived at last, and her tummy was dancing and twirling as energetically as the Sugar Plum Fairy. As she peered out into the midnight frozen mist, a broad smile spread across her face. Her eyes began to sparkle.

She could just make out a particle of light whizzing up and down the street. It came almost to a halt, hovered next to the postbox for a quarter of a moment, before hurtling into the house opposite. She heard a faint noise.

Mrs Andersen smiled. It was happening again. She now knew that this was going to be the best December that young Bruno had ever experienced.

1st December
The Sneeze

It was just before seven when Bruno got out of bed, put on his dressing gown and slippers, and carefully opened his bedroom door. He made his way along the landing when - CREAK- a loud noise came from the floorboard beneath his foot. Bruno stood completely still and held his breath. He had to be totally quiet. He couldn't wake her up before he had completed his mission. A few steps later he reached the door and opened it very slowly. Bruno crept into the room and lightly tiptoed over to the bed. She was still asleep. Her arm was hanging temptingly down over the side of the bed, so he took his chance.

'Pinch, punch, first of the month and no returns!' he called out as he gave her arm a quick nip and a gentle thump with his fist.

'Morning, Mum!' Bruno greeted her to a new day. Mrs Watson opened her eyes sluggishly.

'Good morning, Bruno!' she croaked.

'That's five-two to me!' Bruno announced proudly. 'And it's extra special 'cos it's December now.'

He checked his Spywatch that his father had given him for his birthday that year. 'It's been December in England for exactly six hours and...' he paused as he waited for the seconds to tick on, 'fifty-four minutes.

3

That means it's just twenty-four more sleeps now until… Present Day!'

'Present Day? Oh, Bruno, you mean until *Christmas* Day,' sighed Mrs Watson. 'It's not just about the presents. You know that. There's a lot more to Christmas. Besides, I'm not sure we'll be able to make such a big fuss out of it this year. Money's very tight at the moment.'

'But getting presents is *obviously* the best bit. Everyone knows that!' insisted Bruno. 'And the snow. That's cool, too. Do you think it'll snow this year? It hasn't snowed at Christmas time for ages. I wonder if I'll get a big present from Dad again? Remember, Mum, the huge telly he got me last year?'

'How could I forget?' Mrs Watson said with a weary smile. 'At least it keeps you out of my hair when I'm busy.'

'You're always busy,' Bruno muttered quietly so she wouldn't hear. 'I wonder what he'll get me this year. Something big I hope!'

'Bruno,' Mrs Watson said, changing the subject quickly, 'how about you get me a nice glass of juice and bring it up to me? Help me to wake up.'

Bruno agreed, though he didn't see why she couldn't get one for herself. He trudged down the stairs and into the kitchen, trying to decide what he most wanted for Christmas.

He got out a carton of juice from the fridge and poured a glass for his mum and one for himself. Just as he picked up his mum's glass, he heard what sounded like a sneeze. It made him jump, which then made him spill some of the drink down his pyjamas.

He looked around. They didn't have any pets and there wasn't anyone else in the house apart from Bruno and his mum. Where could the noise have come from? He looked all around the kitchen but he couldn't see anything out of the ordinary.

I wonder what it was? Bruno thought to himself as he peered round the room. He realised there couldn't be anyone else in the kitchen and decided that he must have been hearing things, so he took the drink up to his mum, who noticed the spillage straight away.

'Sorry, Mum. I didn't mean to.'

'No, you never mean to, do you?' Mrs Watson looked at him for a moment. 'Never mind, I was going to do some washing today anyway.'

Bruno huffed. It wasn't his fault he'd spilt the drink. He'd been startled by the noise. He felt like his mum was always quick to point out what he had done wrong, but wasn't so good at praising him when he did something well. But he also knew that his mum was having a tricky time at the moment. He went into his room, got out of his pyjamas and slipped on a clean white t-shirt and a pair of jeans.

Weekends had been much better when his dad had been around. They would play football in the park or go exploring in the woods. But now, Bruno and his mum usually just went shopping, and then she would have loads of chores to do around the house, so he was left on his own. At least he had the telly to watch. He remembered how excited he had been when he opened the massive parcel last Christmas. His dad had even come to deliver it on Christmas Day. He could only stay for an hour, but at least he'd come to see them. He loved his telly, but what he wanted more than anything was a *real* adventure – not just one on a TV screen.

He went back down to the kitchen to get his drink. As he took a gulp, he heard another sneeze and once again spilt juice all down his previously clean white t-shirt.

'Oh, no!' cried Bruno.

Achoo!

Bruno definitely heard a muffled sneeze this time. He looked around the kitchen, but saw nothing that could have made a sneezing sound.

'Anyone there?' he said softly. 'Sounds like you've got a bit of a nasty cold, whoever you are.'

At that moment, his mum walked in. They needed to have breakfast and get ready for the day. Finding out what the mysterious sound was would have to wait.

2nd December
The Biscuit Tin

Bruno headed quietly down to the kitchen. He had tried to stay awake last night until his mum went to bed so that he could investigate further, but he had fallen asleep while waiting.

'Hello? Hell-o-ooo!' he called out in a whisper. 'Anybody there?'

Silence.

He kept perfectly still. Then he heard a faint rustling noise coming from next to the cooker. He crept over. He heard the rustling again. Only this time it sounded more like chomping and he now knew exactly where it was coming from. The biscuit tin! Bruno carefully reached for the tin and gently lifted it up. It was much heavier than usual and as he lifted it, there were muffled cries from inside.

Bruno wondered what it could be. Whatever it was, it had to be pretty small to fit inside a biscuit tin. And then he realised – it must be some kind of a joke. Maybe it was a walkie talkie, or a mobile phone. Perhaps it was his dad trying to make contact with him at last. His face brightened and he tried to prise open the tin. The lid was stiff. He was sure his mum did this deliberately. He was only allowed two biscuits a day,

'To keep you fit as a fiddlestick!' as his mum kept reminding him.

'Dad?' Bruno struggled with the lid until finally, using all his strength, he managed to twist it off. But when he saw what was inside, he didn't know what to think. It certainly wasn't a phone. Bruno stared into the biscuit tin. He'd never seen anything like it.

There appeared to be a very small girl sitting inside the tin, munching on a biscuit. She looked up at him with a smile.

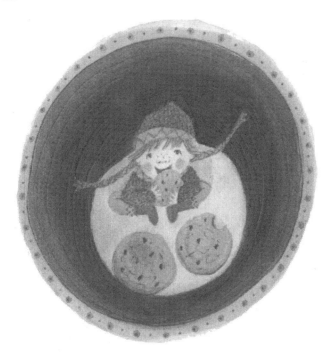

'These cookies is yummy!' she said. 'Very much yummy! How make du dem?'

Bruno didn't quite understand what the small girl meant, so he decided to say nothing.

'Come on! Du can give me secret. So du teach me how you makes the best cookies in the whole world! Old secret resipee, for sure.'

'Resipee?' Bruno repeated. 'Oh, you mean recipe.'

'Yes, but how make du this here cookie? I can really good like the chips of chocolate.'

They were lovely biscuits, but they were just ones they'd got from the supermarket and he told her he didn't know how to make them.

'Wherefore du not knowing? Du just being fjolsy,' she scowled. 'Tell it to me.'

'We didn't make them,' said Bruno. 'We just bought them.'

The small girl looked at him through narrow eyes. 'Du making not your own cookies? This is really wierdulous! Making cookies is one of the best things to do in whole world. Du messiate the kitchen and licky yummy bowl leftovers, and then eat lots of cookies. Du cannot do that if du just *buy* them from a shop.'

Bruno looked at her. She was tiny, but other than that, she looked just like a girl, although her clothes were very old-fashioned, like those he had seen in pictures of Victorian girls. She wore a green floppy Santa hat, but with no bobble at the end.

'Achoo!' she sneezed.

'Bless you!' Bruno said.

'Excuse. I get coldified on journey across sea.'

'Who are you, anyway?' Bruno asked. 'You're way too small to be a person and you sound all funny and say lots of peculiar words.'

The girl opened her eyes wide and gave him a stern stare.

'Sorry,' said Bruno hurriedly, 'I didn't mean to upset you. But what are you doing in my house?'

'I eating cookie,' she explained. 'That what I doing!'

'Yes, I know that,' said Bruno. 'That's not what I meant.'

'Then say du what du mean!' she demanded. 'How can du expect me to knowing what du meaning if du say it not?'

Bruno thought about how best to ask clearly and simply so that the girl would understand him. He could tell that she was not used to speaking English. She was doing really well. He wondered how well he would do if he was somewhere people didn't speak English. He could say hello and say his name and age, and ask for a ham sandwich in French, but that was about it. Not very useful, especially as he didn't even like ham sandwiches. Eventually, he thought of the right words to use.

'What I mean is this: Who are you? What are you? And why are you here?'

And he might have found out, there and then, if he had not heard the creak of a stair. His mum was sleepily making her way to the kitchen.

'Quick, we need to find somewhere for you to hide!' Bruno hissed. But when he looked around, the young girl was nowhere to be seen.

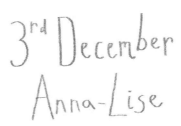

3rd December
Anna-Lise

Early morning seemed to be the only time that his mum was not busying herself about the house, and was therefore the best time for a secret meeting. Bruno checked that his mum was still asleep, before slipping noiselessly down the stairs and into the kitchen. This time he went straight to the biscuit tin and carefully opened it.

'Hello again!' he greeted her as he watched her chomping one of the last biscuits. 'You were going to tell me who and what you are. But we need to be quick, before my mum wakes up.'

The small girl started to laugh. 'Du knows not who I am? Du knows not *what* I am?' Then she looked at him curiously. 'Du *really* not know?'

Bruno had noticed that she kept saying 'Du' instead of 'You' and he thought he'd better let her know.

'I think your English is amazingly good, I really do,' he began carefully, 'but, do you mean *you*, when you say *du*?

The girl bounced her hand off her forehead. 'Self-evidently. Of course. I sorry, yes, I should say, *you*. A thousand thank yous for telling me. I still learning. I try again. *You* really know not what I am?'

13

'That was perfect! But, no, I just know you look like a very small girl, much smaller than any of the girls at school.'

'It is beginning of December and you are not knowing a *nisse* when you see one?'

'A what?'

'A nisse! Nis-se. I am a nisse. You know well what a nisse is, do you not?'

'No!' said Bruno getting frustrated, 'Of course not. I haven't got the foggiest what a *nisse* is, why should I?'

'Because it is December! Christmas month!' exclaimed the girl. 'What whole year is leading to! I can good see you have much to learn, boy. How sad you know not about nisser. I thought everyone knew about us.'

'Well, go on. Tell me then. What is a...a... *nisse*, or whatever you say you are.'

'It is a little difficult to explain if you never have heard of nisser. I suppose you could say I am a sort of... Christmas elf.'

You're kidding! One of Santa's elves?' asked Bruno.

'For sure not! I not work for the Christmas Man. I work for a nisse company. I would not work for the Christmas Man. We have very different ways of thinking about Christmas sometimes. The Christmas Man wants everybody to be good all the time and do nothing wrong. We nisser like to play tricks on people. Especially if they deserve it!'

Bruno stopped to think for a minute. He loved the idea of there being a Father Christmas, but he wasn't quite sure about it. In some of the department stores Santa's beard had looked distinctly fake.

'I think you're lying,' he said, 'I'm not sure there even is a Father Christmas.'

'Oh, really? No Christmas Man? Well, how come I meet him then?' The girl smiled at Bruno who sneered back at her.

'It was probably just some old guy dressed up.'

The girl started laughing again. Only this time it was like she would never stop.

'You really think the Christmas Man is just some old guy dressed up?' she spluttered. 'You really are superfjols! People know about the Christmas Man all over whole world and you not know if you are believing in him?' She was laughing so much that tears were rolling down her cheeks. Bruno was confused, but for some reason, the girl's laughing made Bruno want to laugh and so he began to chuckle, which turned into a snigger and soon they were both falling about laughing. After a while, the nisse managed to get herself back under control.

'If you are really not believing in the Christmas Man, you have even more to learn than I thought!'

Something was puzzling Bruno.

'You keep talking about the Christmas Man. Why don't you just say Father Christmas or Santa?'

'It just another name for same person,' the girl explained. 'We call him the Christmas Man, you call him Father Christmas or Santa or Santa Claus.'

Bruno heard footsteps on the stairs.

'You'd better hide,' he said. 'Don't want my mum seeing you.' He picked up the girl and popped her gently back into the biscuit tin.

'What's your name?' asked Bruno.

'I called Anna-Lise,' she said with a little scowl.

'Anna-Lise, nice to meet you. I'm Bruno. Stay in there and don't make a sound!'

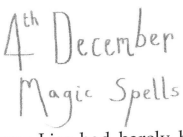

4th December
Magic Spells

Bruno and Anna-Lise had barely had a chance to say good morning to each other when Mrs Watson walked into the kitchen. Bruno clumsily fumbled the lid back on the biscuit tin, with Anna-Lise hidden inside.

'I saw that, Bruno. Don't think I didn't see that.'

Bruno turned around to face his mum, doing his best to hide the biscuit tin.

'Saw what?' He tried to look as innocent as possible.

'Give me the biscuit tin. Now!' demanded his mum.

Bruno knew there was no point arguing when she was in this kind of mood. So, with a feeling of deep dread, his trembling hands gave her the tin, hoping that for some reason she might not open it. But of course, that's exactly what she did. And she was certainly not pleased by what she saw inside.

'And *what* is *this*?' asked Mrs Watson, looking sternly at Bruno. He decided it was probably best to say nothing. Mrs Watson emptied the tin onto the table.

'Careful Mum, you'll hurt her!' he cried.

'What are you talking about, Bruno? Hurt who?' Mrs Watson asked.

Then Bruno looked at the table. All he could see was a half-eaten chocolate chip biscuit. He picked up the tin and looked inside. It was empty. He stared wide-eyed first at the table and then at the empty tin. What was going on? Where had Anna-Lise disappeared to?

'What have you got to say for yourself, Bruno Watson?' demanded his mum. Bruno just stared back at her.

'That tin was half full yesterday,' Mrs Watson continued, 'How many biscuits have you had this morning? I thought I could trust you, but obviously I can't. We agreed your limit is two biscuits a day. Two! It's for your own good. To keep you fit as a fiddlestick. And you have just made a complete pig of yourself!'

Bruno tried to explain that it wasn't him that had eaten all the biscuits, but his mum didn't believe him. Not for a moment.

'And who are you going to tell me it was, then – Father Christmas?'

Not a bad guess, Bruno thought to himself, but he knew his mum well enough not to say it out loud. He could tell her the truth, but what would be the point? He knew there was no way she would believe him if he told her it was a nisse, a kind of Christmas elf, who he had hidden in the biscuit tin, but had somehow magically disappeared. No-one would believe that.

'I don't want to have to do this, Bruno, but you give me no choice. It's upstairs to your room – and no more television! I'm going to take it away and you won't get it back until you've learnt your lesson.'

Bruno had no choice but to accept his punishment, even though he had done nothing wrong. He went up to his room, closed the door and threw himself onto his bed. He didn't realise that he was being watched.

'Unfair!' Bruno yelled into his pillow and punched his duvet with each shout, 'No-fair-no-fair-no-fair!'

Then Bruno heard a faint sound very much like a

This was followed by the sound of a familiar voice.

'It happens many times that life is not fair, Mr Bruno. Life more interesting this way. We just have to dealing with it and carry on.'

Anna-Lise was sitting on one of the shelves of his bookcase, munching a chocolate chip cookie.

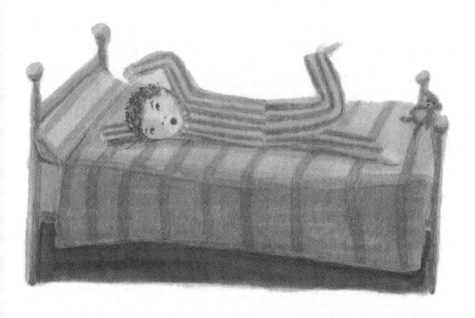

'How did you do that?' asked Bruno.

'Do what?'

'How did you get out of the biscuit tin and onto my bookcase?'

'Easy-peasy!' she said. 'You have heard of magic spelling, yes?'

'Er, kind of...' said Bruno.

'I close my eyes, wish myself upstairs, spell the magic word and… Tral-la!'

'Just like that?' asked Bruno.

'Of course. I spell out D-I-S-A-P-P-E-A-R to make myself disappear, and A-P-P-E-A-R to be seen again. It works in any language, but you have to spell it correctly or it works not. It important for us nisser to be super good at spelling. But I forget – you know not anything about nisser.'

Anna-Lise was about to tell Bruno all about herself, when Bruno heard his mum calling him. They had to leave the house straight away or they would be late.

'It will have to wait until tomorrow,' he sighed, and he went to join his flustered mum.

5th December
The Nisse Hat

Anna-Lise and Bruno were having an early morning chat about her family and friends, when there came a shriek from the bathroom. They both heard footsteps clomping towards them, and the door burst open.

ping

'I suppose you think this is funny!' Mrs Watson cried out to Bruno. Bruno had to try very hard not to laugh. What he saw in front of him *was* very funny indeed. It was, Bruno thought to himself, one of the funniest things he'd ever seen. And even though Anna-Lise had disappeared again, he knew exactly who was responsible.

Bruno stared at his mother, forcing himself not to laugh. Her face was practically purple with rage. Her hair was pointing straight up in a cone shape. Most of it was bright red, with a white border just above her forehead and a white patch at the very tip of her hair.

'Guess you know that your hair looks exactly like a Santa hat, do you Mum?'

'Yes, Bruno,' she said furiously, 'I am aware of that. I don't know how you did it, but I do not find it at all funny. How am I supposed to go out like this?'

'Maybe you could put a real Santa hat on,' Bruno suggested helpfully, 'then that would hide your hair.' 'Don't think you will be getting away lightly with this, Bruno Watson! You are on dishes duty for the next week! Every day!' Mrs Watson slammed the door shut and stormed down the landing to the bathroom and turned on the shower.'

Bruno heard a familiar giggling from the wardrobe. As he opened it, Anna-Lise hopped out with a big smile on her face.

'Your mother, she shall be washing for long time, it take days for hair to get back to normal. No matter how many times she washes. It is not possible to wash out nisse magic!'

'What have you done?' said Bruno. 'I'm in so much trouble now, thanks to you!'

'Yes, I is sorry you in trouble. But she was being un-Christmassy sending you to your room, so I had to do something to make her more Christmassy.'

'But now I've got to do the dishes for a whole week. It's so boring!' Bruno complained.

'You not worry. I help. Do you not think it worth it to see hair like a nisse hat?

'A nisse hat? Don't you mean a Santa hat?'

'Absodefinitely not! We call it a nisse hat because it what we nisser wear.' Anna-Lise pointed to her own

24

hat. 'Many years ago, the Christmas Man saw us wearing them and decided he wanted one of our red ones. So it really a nisse hat, not a Santa hat.'

So playing tricks on people and letting others take the blame is what a nisse does, is it?' Bruno was quite annoyed, although he had to admit that seeing his mum's hair like that was very funny indeed.

'Oh yes,' said Anna-Lise. 'There many more tricks to come. All funny! Nisser are magic. We used to only live in people's lofts. But many people start to live in places without lofts, so we have to find other places to hide. We sometimes play tricks on people, but just fun ones, not nasty. And the nicer the people are to us, the nicer we are to them. Especially if they leave yummicious rice pudding out for us. With much cinnamon.'

'Rice pudding with cinnamon? Is that really your favourite food? More than chocolate?'

'Self-evidently! There nothing better for warming you up on a cold December morning. We come from Scandinavia, where it really cold in winter. You know Scandinavia?'

'Yeah, that's where the Vikings came from.'

Anna-Lise looked around the room. 'You have map?'

'Yes, there's a map of the world on the wall over there.' Bruno picked up Anna-Lise and took her over to the map.

'On map, go from here up to Scotland, turn right and first countries you come to are Scandinavian countries. I from Denmark – this one. It looks a bit like a penguin, you not think?'

'Yeah, I guess it does a bit. Do you have penguins in Denmark, then?'

'No, Denmark is cold in winter, but not that cold. Also, penguins only live on other side of the world. We are in North of the world. And this also where the Christmas Man live. Some people think he live in Lapland, others think he live in Greenland, some even think he live at the North Pole, but nobody really know for sure. He not want too many visitors, so he keep it very secret where he really live.'

'So, if you're from Denmark,' asked Bruno, 'what are you doing in England? Don't you want to be at home?'

'That what I want to talk with you about. I am needing your help,' Anna-Lise said. 'We start tomorrow morning.'

And with a

she was gone.

6ᵗʰ December
ICICLE

'I here because I work for nisse company called ICICLE,' said Anna-Lise.

'ICICLE? That's a cool name!'

'ICICLE is made from first letter of each word of company name.'

'We learnt about that in school. I made the word **BIG**! Bruno Is Great! And what about… *ALICE*.' Bruno exclaimed.

'Who is Alice?' she asked.

'**A**nna Lise **I**s **C**ertainly **E**xcellent! **ALICE**!'

'Oh, I see, yes. Many thank yous, Mr Bruno.'

'But you said you work for *ICICLE*. What does that stand for?' asked Bruno.

'*ICICLE* is 'International Christmas Information Collection and Learning Executive.'

'Wow! That's a long name,' said Bruno. 'I can see why you call it *ICICLE*. What does all that mean?'

'It basically mean we go all around world to find out about Christmas traditions in different countries. And to tell to others about our Christmas traditions in Scandinavia. It so that we can all share the fun things we do and the yummy things we eat at Christmas time. It fun to learn about different countries but it also good to tell about own traditions. We can all learn from each other.'

'That's a cool job,' said Bruno. 'That's what I want to do when I grow up.'

'Unfortunately, this not really possible. Job only for nisser, not for people.'

'That's not fair! But hang on, why do you have a job? You're still a girl. You're not grown up. Shouldn't you be at school?'

'I older than you think,' she said, with a smile.

'How old are you?' Bruno asked.

Anna-Lise stood up on the shelf, holding onto a book for support. 'How old you think I look?' She did a little twirl.

'Dunno. About ten?' Anna-Lise began to laugh uncontrollably.

'Ten! You think I is ten years old?!'

Bruno felt embarrassed. 'Well, I don't know!'

'Excusing me, but you is funny boy, Mr Bruno! You think I ten years old? You really nothing know about nisser at all, do you? A nisse who is ten is only a teeny weeny tiny baby. We live much longer than you humans. I am a young nisse and I is 123 years old.'

'NO WAY! You are NOT 123 years old. That's ridiculous!' said Bruno. 'Nobody is 123 years old.'

'Oh yessy they are, Mr Bruno! Nisser grow much older than people do. Yes, I is 123. I know you think it sound strange, but it true. My father, he is nearly 350 years old. He remembers back many years.'

'350 years old! Wow!' said Bruno, 'I thought my grandma was old but she seems really young now.'

'Anyway,' Anna-Lise continued, 'I have only few weeks and I need your informations.'

'To find out how we celebrate Christmas in England?'

'You right!'

'Why did you choose England? Is it a really good place for Christmas?'

'I not know. That what I here to find out. The ICICLE company give me your address so I come here. They send us to where they think we can find much informations and where we can make somewhere more Christmassy.

'My mum could definitely do with being made more Christmassy!' said Bruno.

'Yes, I think this is perhaps why they send me here. We always sent to a house that needs Christmas hygge.'

'What's that?' Bruno asked.

'You find out before long! It part of my job to make the family Christmassy. And it many years since a member of ICICLE come to England, so the informations is out of date. It was my Aunty Erna.

'Last year,' she continued, 'my friend Jesper, he go to Germany and he loved all the markets and the cakes and drinks. He said there was a wonderful Christmas atmosphere, just as good as being in Denmark for Christmas. But we also get sent to other places that are further away. My sister Camilla, she works also for ICICLE, a few years ago, she went to other side of world to Australia. Christmas very different there.'

Bruno was really curious. 'What's different in Australia?'

'Not tell now. Need to find out about English Christmas now. Tell please!'

'Only if you promise to tell me about Christmas in Australia!' Bruno demanded.

'Yes, I tell you,' she said, 'but later.'

Bruno was annoyed. He hated waiting to find things out. When he wanted to know or do something, he always wanted it straight away. He had never been very good at being patient. But he knew that Anna-Lise would not give in, so he would just have to wait to find out about an Australian Christmas. He started to tell Anna-Lise about all his favourite things that happened at Christmas in England.

7ᵗʰ December
Investigations

Anna-Lise was thrilled to hear all about an English Christmas. There were some things that were just the same as in Denmark, but there were many things that were completely different. She wrote everything she learnt in a small, red, furry notebook so she wouldn't forget any of it.

They talked about English Christmas traditions. They talked so much that Bruno forgot all about not having his telly because he was having so much fun thinking about Christmas. It was great to have someone to talk to. Bruno would set to work on the dirty dishes, but by the time he had washed up the first plate, everything else was mysteriously already clean and on the drying rack. Each time he heard a little voice spelling out 'W-A-S-H U-P' and then a gentle

He would look around, but there was no-one else there. Even so, he always said a quiet 'Thank you' as he knew who it was that had helped him out.

Mrs Watson's hair went back to normal. She had taken to wearing a big woolly hat everywhere she went, even at work. She told everyone that she was feeling the cold and was trying to prevent herself from getting a chill.

Bruno told Anna-Lise about Christmas lights, Christmas trees and advent calendars. They agreed that the best calendars were the ones with chocolates in. Bruno liked his too much to let Anna-Lise have any of the chocolates, though.

'That not friendly, Mr Bruno! Just one choccywoccy?' she pleaded.

'They're my chocolates, Anna-Lise. They're for me!' came the reply from Bruno.

What really interested her were the English traditions that were different from those she was used to. She had never heard of leaving a carrot out for Rudolph (which she thought was a really great idea).

She learnt about all the Christmas food that people have in England, and she was determined to try some in the next couple of weeks. She especially liked the sound of mince pies. Bruno also told her about pantomimes where there is lots of singing and dancing and people being silly and men dressing up as women and girls dressing up as boys, to tell a famous fairytale like *Cinderella* or *Aladdin*.

'We go to Pantomime, yes?' she asked Bruno.

'Unlikely. Mum's not said anything, so probably not this year.'

'Oh, but please! This is my only chance! I can fit in your pocket and see from there. It would be big favour. Will you not ask please?'

'S'pose I can *ask*. We have been to a few different ones. I'd like to go, it was great last time. I went with Mum and Dad. It was *Dick Whittington* and they ended up going on adventures, travelling to Morocco and finding a camel called Mustafa and then going back to London 'cos he heard the bells talking to him.'

'Bells talking to him?'

'Yeah, they said, "Turn again, Whittington, Lord Mayor of London."'

'So he becomes the Mayor of London because some bells tell him this? That sounds completely silliful. Go ask your Mum now. But ask in polite way, yes?'

Bruno did ask his mum. And he was polite. She was reluctant at first as it was quite expensive to go, but when she saw how much he wanted to go, and, impressed that he was asking so nicely, she said she would see. Bruno knew this usually meant no, but he hoped this time it might mean yes.

'Many thank yous for asking, Mr Bruno,' said Anna-Lise. 'It is much nice of you.'

'It's not just for you. I want to go, too! I'd forgotten about pantos until we started talking about them. Actually, I'd forgotten a lot of the cool things about Christmas. We haven't even talked much about the most important bit of Christmas.'

'Now this is very interesting. Because maybe it the same in every country. What is most important thing about Christmas for you, Bruno?'

'I'll tell you in the morning. Time to go to school!'

8th December
Presents

Anna-Lise was not happy with what Bruno had just told her. She shook her head sadly, 'Please say you not think this is true.'

'Of course it's the most important!' said Bruno. 'Getting presents is *easily* the best thing about Christmas! I got a telly last year, and hopefully this year I'll get another big present!'

Anna-Lise looked sad.

'What's wrong?' asked Bruno. 'Everyone wants big presents, don't they?'

'That make me very, very sad,' she said.

'What makes you sad?' Bruno asked. He was confused.

'You think getting presents most important thing about Christmas? Presents good. Of course presents good, but getting presents is very much not most important! I try to learn you this.'

Bruno laughed. 'You won't change my mind! Getting presents is definitely the best thing about Christmas. There's nothing you can say that will make me change my mind!'

'You do know *why* we have Christmas, yes?' she checked.

'Yeah, of course,' said Bruno. 'Jesus was born in a stable at Christmas with animals all around and the wise men came from miles away to give him presents like gold and frankincense and myrrh, but I don't really know what they are, apart from gold. Everyone knows about that story! It's the Nativity story that we are doing for the play at school. And that's why we get presents at Christmas,' Bruno stated confidently. 'Just like Jesus did from the wise men!'

'Always you come back to getting presents. There is more work to do than I first think, but I hope by time I go, you understand what Christmas really about. Not just getting presents on Christmas Eve.'

'What are you talking about? You don't get presents on Christmas Eve!' said Bruno.

Anna-Lise was truly amazed to hear that children in England have to wait until Christmas Day to get their presents. In Denmark, she explained to Bruno, everyone opens their presents on Christmas Eve. The Christmas Man delivers them in the afternoon while the children have a sleep so that they can stay up a bit longer.

Bruno thought about what she had said. After a while, he realised that what she was saying made complete sense.

'I guess he can't be everywhere at once, can he? Even though he is magical. So if he delivers presents on Christmas Eve in Denmark and other countries, he then comes over to England during the night and then we have presents on Christmas morning.'

'Why I not think of this?' asked Anna-Lise, 'You a clever boy, Bruno.'

'But how does he get all the way to Australia? And don't the reindeer get tired after all that flying?' Bruno wondered.

'I tell you about that another day.'

Anna-Lise looked around the room and suddenly had a thought.

'I think something missing! I fix. Back tomorrow!'

And with that, she closed her eyes tight and spelled out 'D-I-S-A-P-P-E-A-R'. She vanished into thin air in front of Bruno's eyes. He wondered where she had gone and what needed fixing.

9th December
Hygge

When Bruno got back from school the next day, he had only seen Anna-Lise for a brief moment, before she disappeared with a smile on her face.

Anna-Lise had been gone several minutes when Bruno heard a quiet noise.

ping

He looked up and Anna-Lise was back.

'It good now. I fix it.'

'What have you fixed? What was wrong?' asked Bruno.

'You will have hygge now!'

'Hygge? What's that?'

'You will find out. It is a lovely feeling. You will like it. You will know it when you feel it.'

There came a call from downstairs.

'Bruno Watson, get down here this instant!' his mum demanded.

He glared at Anna-Lise. 'You'd better not have got me in trouble again!'

Anna-Lise giggled. Bruno went down the stairs nervously. What had she done this time? As he went into the living room he saw his mum with her arms folded standing next to a large, undecorated Christmas tree.

'What have you got to say for yourself, young man?' asked Mrs Watson sternly.

By now, Bruno was learning to think quickly. He'd had to take the blame for Anna-Lise's actions ever since she'd arrived. So far, he'd just about got away with it, but this was one thing he couldn't pretend wasn't there. The tree was right in front of him.

'Where did you get this from? You haven't been stealing, have you?' Mrs Watson demanded.

'Course not!' said Bruno, madly trying to think of what to say to his mum. He couldn't very well say that a nisse had conjured it here, but he also didn't want to lie to his mum.

'I didn't steal it,' he said carefully. 'Let's just say I've been saving my pocket money.' It was true. He had been saving his pocket money.

'Spending your own money on a tree? You don't need to do that. We usually go and get the tree just before Christmas. Was it just that you couldn't wait?'

'Something like that,' he said. 'It's nice to have it in here for more of December, isn't it?'

'It does make the room a little more festive, I suppose. But it just won't do.'

Bruno's heart sank. Now that he'd got over the shock of having to try to explain why the tree was there, he thought it looked great, and he wanted it to stay. He was sad to think that his mum wanted to take it away.

'It certainly won't do,' she said, 'to have a Christmas tree looking so bare. I think we need to find the decorations, don't you? We can decorate it together.'

Bruno's eyes lit up. He loved decorating the tree, but last year he'd had to do it by himself. It would be much more fun to do it together with his mum. They found the Christmas box up in the attic and they had a great time hanging baubles and little Christmas figures all over the tree. Bruno was responsible for the bottom half and his mum hung things on the branches near the top. Before long the tree was glistening in many different colours. They had found the decorations that they had collected over many years, and as a result the tree gleamed in gold, silver, red, blue and purple.

When they were nearly finished, Mrs Watson went to make them a congratulatory hot chocolate.

'Psst!' came a small voice. 'Hey, Bruno, you has forgotten the star!'

'What star?' whispered Bruno.

'For the top of the tree of course.'

'We don't have a star on the top. We're gonna put the fairy on the top of the tree. And we haven't forgotten her, it's always the last thing we put on the tree when everything else is done.'

'This is much interesting. A fairy instead of a star on top of the tree. I can good like it,' and Anna-Lise made a note in her book which was already getting full of interesting English Christmas facts.

Mrs Watson came back in.

'I do love hot chocolate,' she said, 'but we've nearly run out. Remind me to get some more, Bruno. I always forget.'

Decorating the tree had put Mrs Watson in a Christmassy mood. She used all her strength to lift Bruno up so he could place the fairy onto the top of the tree. She turned on the fairy lights that were draped on the tree, and they stood back and admired their work. The tree looked fantastic. But Mrs Watson wasn't satisfied.

'Bruno, our work has only just begun,' she said. Bruno noticed a glint in her eye. He hadn't seen her this happy for ages.

'Guess what we are going to do after our mince pies,' she said.

They spent the evening decorating the whole house. They went into the garden where Bruno chose some holly for his mum to cut and place all around the house. They hung up silver and gold tinsel everywhere, and soon the whole house was looking beautifully festive. Bruno went to bed that evening feeling tired but very happy. It had been such a fun day, but most importantly, he'd had a really good time with his mum. He couldn't remember the last time they had spent a whole evening together just having fun. He thought back to the strange word Anna-Lise had told him earlier. *Hygge*. He was certain that he had experienced *hygge* with his mum that evening.

He found himself looking forward to what the next day would bring. He'd already had amazing adventures, but it wasn't even halfway through December yet. He knew that with Anna-Lise around, the adventures were bound to continue. Bruno's dreams that night were full of Christmas trees and reindeer and snow.

10th December
Peppernuts

Bruno was getting ready for school, packing his lunchbox with the sandwich his mother had made, a satsuma, a carton of apple juice and a mince pie.

'What is this round thing?' asked Anna-Lise who was sitting on the biscuit tin.

'That's a mince pie. Remember, I told you about them when you first arrived?'

'Yes, I remember. I try some?' she asked. Bruno peeled a little piece off and handed it to her. She took a handful and shoved it in her mouth. Crumbs went everywhere.

'But this is tastilicious! Yum-my! Nearly as good as peppernuts. You have tasted peppernuts?'

'Peppernuts?' Bruno didn't know what they were. 'That sounds horrible.'

'Very much not horrible! Little sweet cookies with Christmassy spices in. We make some when you back from school. We need kitchen when your mother busy.'

'That shouldn't be a problem,' grumbled Bruno, 'she's nearly always busy doing something.'

When he got back from school, his mother had some things to take care of.

'Bruno, I need you to promise not to disturb me for the next few minutes unless it's very, very important.'

'Okay, Mum.' This was perfect. She didn't want him to disturb her, and he didn't want her to disturb him. He rushed downstairs. Anna-Lise was already holding the apron up for him to wear.

'You will get much messy, so put this on. We need flour, sugar, butter, eggs, baking soda, vanilla, cinnamon, cardamom, cloves and allspice. Fetch please.'

Bruno went round the kitchen finding the ingredients. He found everything except the cardamom and placed them all on the kitchen table.

'Oki doki. We have to make without cardamom. Now follow my directions,' said Anna-Lise. Bruno did as he was told. He mixed together the butter and sugar in a bowl. Then he beat in the eggs one at a time. He mixed up the flour and cinnamon and stirred it into the sugar mixture until it was all blended.

'You nicely messy! Well done! Good baking!' exclaimed Anna-Lise. Bruno looked at himself. There was almost as much mixture on the apron as there was in the bowl. 'Now to roll it!'

Bruno divided the dough into smaller dough balls and rolled each one into a long thin rope.

Carefully, instructed by Anna-Lise, he then cut each rope into lots of tiny balls and finally placed dozens of them onto a baking tray.

'You had better get hold of your mother. Next part needs oven.' Bruno went upstairs and found the door to her study firmly closed. He put his ear to the door and listened. He could hear just a few muffled words.

'That's great … thank you … and you'll send them in the post? … Thanks, goodbye.' There followed a click. Bruno guessed that his mum had put the phone down, so he knocked on the door and opened it.

'I thought I told you not to disturb me. How long have you been there?'

'Just got here,' he explained. 'You said fifteen minutes. It's been about fifteen minutes and I need you for something. I didn't think you'd want me to put things in the oven, so I've come to ask you to do it.'

'And just what is it that we're putting in the oven?' Mrs Watson was curious but Bruno wouldn't tell her. He wanted her to see for herself and he led her down to the kitchen. She stood staring at the baking tray for a moment and a smile slowly spread across her face.

'Peppernuts. You've made peppernuts!'

Bruno was astonished. 'How do you know about peppernuts?' he asked.

'Do you know, I've no idea. But as soon as I saw them, I knew exactly what they were. I haven't seen these since I was a little girl.'

'That must have been about a million years ago,' joked Bruno cheekily.

'It does sometimes feel like a million years ago. Come on, let's put these in the oven. In no time at all they'll be cooked and we'll have the smell of Christmas all through the house.'

Mrs Watson seemed even more excited about it that Bruno did. He liked seeing his mum smiling and relaxed – it made him feel happy and content.

After about ten minutes, just as Mrs Watson had predicted, the air was filled with the smell of Christmas spices. They took the peppernuts out of the oven and left them to cool. That evening, after dinner, they each had a cup of cocoa and nibbled on peppernuts.

This is hygge! Bruno thought to himself. It had been a wonderful week for Bruno. He couldn't wait for the next one to begin. He wanted Anna-Lise to stay for ever.

11th December

Cards

There was an envelope bearing his name lying on the kitchen table when Bruno got home from school. It was handwritten, not typed, in old-fashioned writing, so he quickly guessed who it was from. He wondered what was inside so he took the envelope up to his room and sat down on his bed. Out of the corner of his eye he spied Anna-Lise munching a biscuit.

'What is it you have?' she asked with her mouth half full.

'A letter from you!' said Bruno.

'Nopey. Nothing to do with me. I have day of writing things about English Christmas in my book.'

'But if the letter isn't from you, then who is it from? No-one ever sends me letters. We get e-mails sometimes from family, but not letters.'

Anna-Lise explained to Bruno that she loved getting post. She thought it was more fun than silly modern e-mails and texts. She didn't understand why people now like these telephones they always carry. Why didn't they just use bananas that glow? That's what Anna-Lise and her family did. Bruno didn't quite understand but he nodded anyway.

'It always exciting to find out what inside a letter,' she said. 'Something you can hold, not just on screen. Now, there is only one way to find out who it from...' she said before stuffing a small piece of biscuit in her mouth.

Bruno tore open the envelope excitedly. It was a card. It had a picture of an old village covered in snow, with some children playing in the snow. He realised it must be a Christmas card. But he never normally got Christmas cards. Sometimes at school, children gave each other cards, but he wasn't usually sent one in the post. The family got sent cards, but he'd never before had a card sent just to him. It made him feel special and gave him a warm, glowing feeling inside.

He opened the card. It wasn't easy to read as the handwriting was all curly. He concentrated hard and managed to guess some words that he wasn't sure about.

'What says it? What says it?' Anna-Lise cried out excitedly.

'I'm pretty sure it says: *Dear Bruno, Have a wonderful Christmas and a very Happy New Year. Perhaps I will see more of you next year. Thinking of you. Lots of love, Grandma.*'

'This lovely,' smiled Anna-Lise. 'She like you much and want to spend more time with you.'

'It's always fun at Grandma's. She gives me loads of sweets and we play games. It's ages since we went there, though. Maybe I'll ask Mum if we can see her soon.'

'That sound a good idea. You can good like getting card?'

'Yeah, it's nice to have a card that's just for you. I'd forgotten about how fun it is when we go to Grandma's.'

'Maybe she like to hear from you.'

'We could text her, I s'pose.'

'Or...' suggested Anna-Lise, 'what you think she like even more?'

'Of course!' said Bruno. 'I could send her a Christmas card.'

'I think she like this very much.' Anna-Lise was pleased with Bruno's idea.

And so Bruno made a card for his Grandma. He found a piece of card and his crayons and drew a picture of a stripy stocking with small presents coming out of the top. When he showed it to Anna-Lise, she looked puzzled.

'Er, it very nice, Mr Bruno, but why you draw picture of a smelly sock? Not very Christmassy.'

'It's a stocking, not a sock!'

'A stocking? What is that?'

'It's kind of a long sock. You hang it up on Christmas Eve and in the morning, Santa's filled it with little presents and sometimes a piece of fruit like a satsuma and usually a coin. I got a pound coin last year.'

'This Christmas tradition?'

'Yes, of course! Don't you hang up a stocking?' asked Bruno.

'I not have before, but think I will this year,' said Anna-Lise. Sounds a great idea. I approve muchly!'

Bruno wrote a message in the card to his Grandma and signed it. When he handed it to his mum to send it for him, she was surprised that he had done it, but really pleased.

'Well done, Bruno! That was a really kind thing to do,' his mum told him.

Bruno spent the evening making cards for his Mum, Dad, and some of his friends at school. Anna-Lise helped out with a few suggestions for drawings. It was much easier for her to make cards. She just closed her eyes and spelt out C-A-R-D. As Bruno made the cards, he thought about how good it had felt to get a card and how happy people would be to get a card from him.

Bruno switched out the light as he settled under his duvet.

'Psst. Bruno!' Anna-Lise's voice whispered.

'What?' he whispered back.

'Know you about Santa Lucia?'

'Is that who Santa is married to?'

'No silly! Santa Lucia is from many years ago. I tell you all about her tomorrow.'

12th December
Special Days

That morning, as soon as Bruno got up, he searched for Anna-Lise, but she was nowhere to be found. Reluctantly, he went to school without having found out about this Santa Lucia person that Anna-Lise had mentioned. He was convinced it must be some relative of Santa Claus.

All day he found it difficult to concentrate in class because he was thinking so much about it. He really wanted to know who Santa Lucia was.

Once he got home, he dashed upstairs, but he found his room in total darkness. The curtains had been drawn and the light wouldn't switch on.

'Come and sit down, Mr Bruno,' said a familiar voice from the darkness. 'You learn now about Santa Lucia.'

'At last! Where were you this morning?' asked Bruno.

'In morning I prepare for now. So, we begin. But first I want to know something. Do you know about any special days at this time of year?'

'Apart from Present Day and…'

Anna-Lise gave him a stern stare.

'Sorry. I mean, apart from *Christmas* Day and Boxing Day, you mean?' asked Bruno.

'Yes, they too obvious,' Anna-Lise said, pleased that Bruno had corrected himself.

'Well, I know there's Hannukah. That's the Jewish festival. But I think that happens over many different days. You definitely get presents on lots of different days, which is pretty cool.'

'Any others?'

'We learnt at school about Divali. I think it's a Hindu festival of light.'

Anna-Lise's face lit up.

'Festival of light? But this is like Santa Lucia!'

'Are you going to tell me what Santa Lucia is then?'

'Absodefinitely!' Anna-Lise pointed her finger at a small candle with a look of concentration on her face and started spelling out some letters.

'F-L-A-I-M'

But nothing happened.

'This very frustrating,' she said. 'I spell but it not happen.'

Bruno looked puzzled. 'What are you trying to spell?' he asked.

'Flaim! What you get when you light candle, you get flaim,' she replied.

Bruno looked very pleased with himself. 'I know why nothing happened,' he said proudly. 'You're spelling it wrong. It's F-L-A-M-E.'

'Many thank yous, Mr Bruno,' the nisse exclaimed. 'This explains the problem. Hokey-pokey. I try again.' She pointed her finger at the candle again and spelled out F-L-A-M-E. At once, the candle was lit with a little glowing flame.

'Santa Lucia was a saint in Italy, many years ago. I guess her English name would be St Lucy, but her name, Lucia, means *light* in Italian. She live in Roman times and helped Christian people who were starving because the Romans stopped them getting food.

'There different stories about what she did. One story is that one night a ship came with food for starving people. Santa Lucia was at front of ship, with a glow around her head to light the way. Another story is that she helped to get food to Christians hiding in catacombs underground who were hiding from Romans. She had candles to help light the way in the darkness.'

'Wow! She sounds amazingly brave. But what has that got to do with December?'

'In Scandinavia, we celebrate and remember her good deeds on 13th December.'

'That's tomorrow!'

'Yes! This means, tomorrow, in each place, a girl is chosen to be Santa Lucia and she leads procession, dressed in white with candles on her head and everyone sings a song. There are many grown-ups there too, so they make sure it all safe. Not safe to put candles on head if not grown-ups around.'

'Sounds fun. But does it have to be a girl?'

'Yes, of course it have to be a girl. Always. This is tradition. Lucia was girl. But there is something boys can do to celebrate.'

'Really? What?' Bruno looked wide-eyed at Anna-Lise. He was determined to do something to celebrate the day.

'Well, in morning on 13th December, children take breakfast to parents in bed, just like Santa Lucia bring food and drink to people she helping many years ago.'

'So, it's remembering what she did by doing the same nice thing for someone else?'

'Defilutely!'

'But why can't my mum bring breakfast to *me*?' said Bruno.

Anna-Lise gave him a look he was starting to know quite well. She was not impressed.

'Bruno,' she began, 'how many times your mother makes you breakfast, lunch and dinner and all your other meals.'

'Pretty much every day, I guess,' he said.

'And how many times you make her a meal?'

Bruno thought for a moment. 'Can't remember. Don't think I have, really.'

'Well, this is good chance to do a nice thing for your mother. For you to give breakfast to her for once, instead of other way round.'

Bruno knew she was right. He went to bed early that night, still forming a plan in his head for the morning. His mother had no idea what lay in store for her the next day.

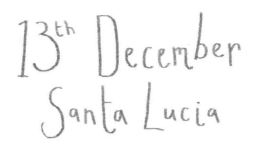

13ᵗʰ December
Santa Lucia

Bruno got up especially early that morning and made his way down to the kitchen before his mother had even woken up. He was determined to start Santa Lucia Day in the proper way. He filled a bowl with cereal and added a little milk.

'How about glass of juice, too?' suggested Anna-Lise, helpfully. She had also got up early. She wanted to make sure that Bruno remembered about taking breakfast to his mother. But he had not needed reminding.

Bruno poured some orange juice into a glass and put the glass onto a tray. He then placed the bowl onto the tray and lifted the whole thing. Now for the tricky bit. He knew he had to be very careful. He suddenly remembered a scene in a pantomime he saw a few years ago.

'I hope I don't end up like Wishy Washy?'

'Wishy Washy? Who is this? This very silly name! I like it!'

'He's Aladdin's best friend. There was this one point when they were making custard pies and the cream and gunk ended up going all over him. I hope Mum's breakfast doesn't end up all over me!'

'Better be very careful in taking it up stairs, then,' warned Anna-Lise, her eyes fixed on him. He carried the tray over to the bottom of the stairs, and he started to climb them, very slowly. He didn't want to drop anything. When he had reached the fifth step he noticed the bowl starting to glide to the right. Very calmly, he stopped where he was and lifted the right side of the tray very slightly and the bowl stopped moving.

Eventually, after what seemed like ages to Bruno, he had almost reached the top of the stairs when he caught his foot on the top step. The tray flew up into the air. Bruno feared the worst. He desperately lunged to catch the tray but he fell face down onto the landing. He waited for the crashing sound. He knew that he would end up like Wishy-Washy after all and was really upset that all his good work had come to nothing. He closed his eyes tight and put his hands over his ears and waited for the sound of the tray to come crashing down.

But the crash never came.

He cautiously opened his eyes and looked at the ground. There was no sign of the tray. When he looked up he could hardly believe his eyes.

The tray was hovering in mid-air with the cereal and the juice unspoilt. It didn't take him long to realise that someone had helped out with a little nisse magic.

'Phew, that was a close one. Thanks, Anna-Lise!' he whispered. Bruno stood up and carefully took hold of the tray, suspended in mid-air, and carried it to the door of his mother's bedroom. He put the tray down on the floor and knocked loudly. He wanted it to seem like room service in a hotel to make it extra special. He heard a sleepy voice coming from inside.

'Bruno? Is something wrong?' came his mother's voice.

'No, Mum. Nothing's wrong. In fact, I have a surprise for you.' And with that he opened the door, picked up the tray and took it over to his mother.

'Happy Santa Lucia Day, Mum!' Mrs Watson looked at him.

'Happy what?'

'Santa Lucia Day! It's a Scandinavian Festival Day when girls have candles on their heads and parents get breakfast in bed!' Mrs Watson still looked unconvinced.

'It's true, Mum!'

'Well, I can't say I've ever heard of it...' She paused. 'But I like the idea very much. I think it is a tradition we should keep every year. At least the breakfast in bed part. I'm not so sure about candles on heads. I could get used to this.' Mrs Watson tucked into her cereal and sipped her orange juice.

'This is lovely. Thank you, Bruno. It's very kind of you.' Bruno was filled with pride. It wasn't often he made his mother this happy, but it was a really good feeling.

'As a reward, I'm going to let you have your telly back. It's in the cupboard.'

'Cool! Thanks mum!' As he opened the cupboard door a thought came into his head. 'Actually, could I ask for something else instead?'

Mrs Watson looked at him suspiciously. 'You mean there is something you want more than your telly? Are you feeling alright?'

'I'm feeling more than alright.' Just a few weeks ago, there was nothing Bruno liked more than watching his TV. Mrs Watson was amazed. What on earth could it be that he wished for?

Bruno caught a glimpse of Anna-Lise out of the corner of his eye. He winked at her and she grinned the widest smile he had ever seen. She knew what he was going to ask for and it filled her with happiness. But she would have to wait for a few days more.

14th December
Carol Singing

At half past five, Mrs Watson called upstairs to Bruno. 'I need you to be ready to go out in half an hour. Don't forget we're going to the town square.'

'What happening in town square?' asked Anna-Lise.

'It's the Carols in the Square this evening,' Bruno replied.

The nisse looked at Bruno with surprise. 'Why you go to see many women called Carol?' she asked. 'Is they very nice?'

'No, Silly!' Bruno laughed, 'It's Christmas Carols, not ladies called Carol. You know, old-fashioned Christmas songs!'

Anna-Lise burst into a fit of giggles. 'Of course! I silly! But this sound magnififul. I love Christmas songs! I very much want to go. I hide in your pocket, yes?'

Bruno shrugged his shoulders. 'Guess so. It's quite fun, but it's the same every year.'

'But that one of the best bits about Christmas. Things should be the same. It is tradition.'

'S'pose,' agreed Bruno.

'What your favourite Christmas song?' asked Anna-Lise. 'We've got loads of different ones back home. You have too?'

'Don't really have a favourite. There's so many. Tons and tons of Christmas songs.'

'What like?'

'There's *Last Christmas*. That's by a band called *Wham*.'

'Excusing me? A music group calls itself *Wham*? This magtastic silly name!'

'Most of the pop songs are really old, like from the 70's and 80's.'

'This, Bruno, is not old to a nisse who is 123 years old.'

'Guess not. What else? There's the one that goes *I wish it could be Christmas every day*.'

'This great! I also sometimes wish every day was Christmas.'

'There's the really old songs like *Frosty the Snowman*, *White Christmas* and *Chestnuts Roasting on an Open Fire*.' Anna-Lise's face glowed with the thought of roasted chestnuts.

'This is your traditional Christmas songs?' she asked.

'Well, sort of, yeah. Course, the most traditional are Christmas carols. That's what we're gonna sing tonight. *Away in a Manger*, *Deck the Halls*, *Little Donkey*, *Silent Night*, all that lot.'

'*Silent Night*? This maybe same as in Germany,' she guessed. 'They have song that goes: *Quiet night, Holy night.*'

'Yeah, sounds like it's pretty much the same as our song.'

Bruno and his mum set off for the town square. If you had looked very carefully, you could just have seen the top of a small green hat popping out of Bruno's pocket.

By the time they arrived at the square, there were already over a hundred people gathered around a brass band that was playing *Good King Wenceslas*.

As the band played the carols, everyone joined in the songs they knew and sang the parts of songs that they knew some of, and hummed and 'La-la'ed the rest. There was one lady who was singing very enthusiastically even though she only seemed to know about half the words.

A kind-looking old lady approached them with a gentle smile.

'Merry Christmas to all three of you,' she said.

Mrs Watson looked confused.

'Thank you, Mrs Andersen, but there's only two of us now.'

'Yes, of course. My mistake.' But with a knowing smile she turned to Bruno and gave him a bag full of peppernuts.

'These are homemade. They are for you and anyone who might want to share them with you.' She glanced at his pocket and then back at Bruno. 'Have a wonderful Christmas.' And with that she walked into the crowd and disappeared.

'Do you think she saw you?' whispered Bruno.

'Nopi-dopi,' Anna-Lise replied. 'How could she? Anyway, she is friendly. Peppernuts! Yum-tum-ti-tum!'

Anna-Lise looked around and among the happy, smiling people she noticed a sour-faced girl. She saw her talking to her parents.

'This is stupid,' the girl moaned. 'Why do we have to come and do this every year? They're just silly old songs and it's cold and why couldn't I just stay at home and watch telly? Where's my mince pies? You *promised* I could have lots of mince pies!'

Anna-Lise noted how un-Christmassy this girl was being and decided she needed teaching a lesson. As she was deciding what to do, a smile started to spread across her face and she let out a little giggle.

After a few minutes, there was a pause in the singing, and people dressed in hats and scarves began to hand out steaming cups of mulled wine to the adults and hot chocolate to the children. Bruno waited patiently for his hot chocolate. He was glad of it when it came. He was just starting to feel a bit chilly, but a few sips later he felt snug and warm again, holding the cup with both mittens. He heard a faint *ping*, followed soon after by a scream from the other side of the square.

'Urgh! Yuk. Yuk. YUK! That's gross!' screamed the girl, spitting food out of her mouth. 'Daddy! I don't know what this is supposed to be, but it's certainly not a mince pie!' Her father tried to calm her down, but to his horror, when he looked at her face, he saw that her nose was getting rounder and rounder and was beginning to flash bright red.

Everyone in the square was watching her now and laughing at her nose. They all thought it must be a plastic nose that she had put on. But soon her face was covered in a brown fur and antlers were sprouting from the top of her head. Her nose kept flashing on and off, on and off. People began to laugh even more as they thought it must be a joke. When the girl's parents saw what was happening, however, they dragged her away from the square to find out what was happening to their daughter. Bruno knew exactly who was responsible.

'What did you put in her mince pie, Anna-Lise?' he asked.

Through her giggling, she told him. 'Oh, I just point my finger and turn her mince pie into magic reindeer food. It make her head turn into Rudolph just for an hour or two. Then she back to her silly normal self. She was being too un-Christmassy. I not like her being so spoilt, so I teach her a lesson.'

The singing started again and everyone had a wonderful time. Anna-Lise knew a few of the tunes, and joined in the singing, and they all went home with a warm, fuzzy feeling inside.

15th December
The Snow Girl

'Wow!' shouted Bruno. 'It's beautiful!' Outside, the trees were glistening and tiny icicles were hanging from anything they could cling onto. He could just make out an area of the garden where the snow had been disturbed. A small figure was moving around in the snow. Bruno wanted to go and investigate, so he quickly slipped on a pair of trousers, a warm woolly jumper and ran downstairs. He grabbed his coat, pulled on his hat, mittens and boots, and flung open the door.

A burst of cold air greeted him as he leapt outside but he didn't mind. He trudged carefully through the snow, enjoying the squeaking sound his footsteps made as the snow was crushed under his boots. He soon decided that he was going too slowly, however, so he started to jump through the snow with both feet together, pretending he was a kangaroo.

'Woo-hoo!' he shouted as he bounced around the garden. He remembered that Anna-Lise had promised to tell him all about Christmas in Australia. He made a mental note to remind her.

Then he spotted her. She was rolling around in the snow, having a wonderful time. Bruno grabbed a bit of snow and made a mini snowball. He didn't want to hurt her, but the chance was too good to miss. He threw the mini snowball straight at her. It made her shriek with delight.

'Bruno! You is up! I been waiting for you to wake up. Isn't this fantasmagorical? Snow is a nisse's bestest weather. I so happy! Now you is here, we can do what I been wanting to do since I awake.'

'What's that?' asked Bruno.

'It what *everyone* want to do as soon as they see much snow. What is the thing *you* most want to do, Bruno?'

'A snowman!' Bruno shouted out. 'Yes, let's make a snowman!'

So Bruno and Anna-Lise set about making a snowman. Bruno gathered up clumps of snow and put them all in a pile, squashing the snow together every now and then. Anna-Lise used a little Nisse Magic to double the amount of snow that Bruno had picked up. But after ten minutes they still had not got very far. The snowman had hardly begun to take shape.

As he was gathering some more snow, Bruno felt a thud in the middle of his back. He turned round to find that his mother was outside, laughing and pointing at him.

'What a great shot!' she yelled. 'I'm the snowball throwing champion!'

'Oh yeah? Wanna bet?' Bruno formed a large ball of snow in his mittens. 'If you think your shot was good, what about *this* one?'

He threw the snowball at his mother. She turned round to avoid it, but it hit her directly on her bottom, and she gave out a yelp.

'I'll get you for that!' she said, laughing. And on they went throwing snow at each other. Sometimes they hit, other times they missed completely, but they didn't seem to care. When they were both exhausted, lying in the snow, Mrs Watson saw the partially made snowman.

'Call that a snowman? Come on, let's finish him.'

Mrs Watson picked up the lump of snow that Bruno had made and started rolling it. She got Bruno to help her roll it around the garden. Snow was sticking to the lump as they rolled it and it got bigger and bigger. Once the lump was big enough, they left it in the middle of the garden and set about making another, smaller lump. They both used all of their strength to lift the smaller lump onto the big one.

'That's more like it,' said Mrs Watson. 'Now he looks like a proper snowman. Except there's something missing. You find some small stones, Bruno. I'll be back in a minute.'

Bruno wandered around the garden looking for little pebbles. The garden looked fun now. The bushes were still covered in snow and icicles hung from the trees, but there were zig-zag patterns of muddy green where they had rolled the snow. He found a few little stones, and his mother soon returned from inside.

'Here we go,' she said, 'this should make him look much better.' Bundled in her arms, she had a bright, colourful scarf, an old hat and a carrot. Together they wrapped the scarf around the neck of the snowman, placed the hat on top of the head and inserted the carrot into the middle of the face. Bruno pushed the pebbles into the face to make a pair of eyes and a big smiling mouth.

'Now for the final, important moment in making a snowman,' Mrs Watson announced. 'What are we going to call him?' Bruno thought for a minute.

'Does it have to be a snow*man*? Couldn't it be a snow*woman* or a snow*girl*?' asked Bruno.

'It's usually a snowman, but I don't see why it couldn't be a snowgirl. Quite right, Bruno. What shall we call her?' Bruno smiled as an idea came into his head.

'Let's call her Anna-Lise,' he suggested.

'Anna-Lise? That's an unusual name,' said Mrs Watson, but I think it's lovely. Yes, we shall call her Anna-Lise! Now let's see if we've got any hot chocolate to warm ourselves up.'

As they went inside, the little nisse watched on, perched on a branch. She jumped down and looked up proudly at the snowgirl that shared her name. Her finger pointed at the snowgirl, and if you had listened very carefully, you would have heard a faint

as Anna-Lise used a little nisse magic.

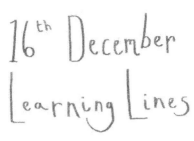

16th December
Learning Lines

During the next day, the snow slowly melted, the roads turned to brown slush, and Bruno was back at school. When he came home, however, he noticed that the snowgirl was still standing tall. While everything else had melted, the snowgirl was just as big as when they had made her the day before.

'Weird,' he thought to himself as he went inside. He went straight up to his room and got out his script for the school play. They were performing it tomorrow and had been rehearsing for the last week, but he had found it really difficult to remember his lines. Therefore, he was going over and over them in his head, hoping that somehow they would stick in his brain. He'd tried putting them under his pillow at night. He thought that they might magically be absorbed into his head, but it hadn't worked.

'What you reading, Mr Bruno?' asked Anna-Lise, who was sitting on the bookcase. Bruno had got so used to having her around that he sometimes forgot to say hello to her when he saw her.

'Sorry, Anna-Lise. Didn't notice you there. I was concentrating so much on learning my lines.'

'You is learning lines? This sounds very strange to me. Is they straight lines or curved lines? Maybe wavey lines?' asked the nisse.

'No, not that sort of lines. That would be really easy to learn.'

'Then what mean you?'

Bruno explained to her about the school play and how they had to remember the words they had to speak.

'When is you performing? And what is the play?' she asked.

'It's called *A Baby in Bethlehem* and we're performing it tomorrow!' said Bruno miserably. 'It's really fun to do, except I keep forgetting what I'm supposed to be saying.'

'Why not I help you? What part you playing?'

'I wanted to be a donkey, but they made me play a shepherd. I have to wear a woolly jumper and a tea-towel on my head.'

'This sound great! Read me your lines.'

'Can't you just use a bit of magic to let me remember them?'

'Mr Bruno! I shocked! This would be cheating. With a bit of hard work I know you can do it. Come, we begin. Show me the words.' And so they went through the script, stopping at all the places where Bruno had some words to say. Anna-Lise was very strict and made sure he could say the lines word perfectly before they moved on to the next bit.

'Look, there the kings go!' said Bruno.

Anna-Lise corrected him. 'Not quite but nearly. It is 'Behold, there go the kings!'

'Oh, ok. Behold, there go the kings!'

'Brilltastic! That was perfect. One more time so you know it super well.'

'Do I have to?'

The stare from the nisse told him that he did have to. And so they went on, through the whole script. Bruno had five things to say, and by dinnertime, thanks to Anna-Lise's help, he was pretty sure he knew all of them.

'But what if I forget them tomorrow?'

'You won't forget them. Just enjoy doing the show,' said Anna-Lise.

'It's a shame you won't be able to see it,' said Bruno, but I'll tell you all about it tomorrow after school. But Anna-Lise had other ideas.

17th December
Christmas Play

Nobody noticed a tiny girl making her way down the street in the early afternoon. At least *almost* nobody noticed. Anna-Lise thought she detected the twitch of a curtain at the window of the house opposite. But when she looked closer, she couldn't see anyone, shrugged her shoulders and carried on.

The only thing she had to watch out for was dogs. For some reason, dogs nearly always seem to notice nisser and feel they have a right to go up to them and sniff them all over. But they never do any real harm, though Anna-Lise remembered what her sister Nina had told her. Once, when Nina was out investigating acorns in a wood, a dog had approached and she had quickly hidden in a bush. The dog had come to the bush, not noticing her at all. It had lifted its leg and weed all over her without realising she was there. She'd had a very long bath in a pond after that had happened.

Anna-Lise was keen to avoid that happening today. Every now and then, she spotted a dog approaching. She would quickly hide in the nearest bush, and climb up as high as possible.

Luckily, the dogs all seemed friendly today. The worst thing that happened was that she was given a lick by a labrador. It wasn't very pleasant, but she remembered what had happened to Nina and counted herself lucky.

After a few minutes of dodging dogs, Anna-Lise found herself at her destination. *Welcome to Appleton Primary School*, the sign read. She sneaked her way through the playground and into the school building.

The school was buzzing with excitement today. She peeked into classrooms as she went past. Children were putting on a fantastic array of costumes. Some had crowns on their head, others had animal masks and she recognised the shepherds by their woolly jumpers and tea-towels. Finally, she reached a big room with lots of chairs set out in rows.

'This must be it,' she said to herself. 'Now to find the best place to see from.' She looked around and decided that for somebody her size, the best place would be up high. So she climbed up the gym bars and sat in a hoop near the top. She knew that she would see everything that happened in the show.

Before long, people started to enter the hall and sit down. The noise and excitement levels got bigger and bigger until the music started and everyone's chatter died down to concentrate on what was happening.

The show was wonderful. The children all performed fantastically and their voices were loud and clear so Anna-Lise could hear every word, even high up on the gym bars.

She especially liked the dancing camels and the songs, but the part she enjoyed the most was when Bruno came on. She let out a little squeal of delight to see him, but quickly put her hand over her mouth. Thankfully, nobody heard her.

She wished now that she could use some nisse magic to help Bruno remember his lines, but knew that would be cheating. So, she crossed her fingers and hoped that Bruno got his first line right and held her breath when she knew it was coming.

'Behold, there go the kings!' she heard him say. Phew, he'd got that one right. She saw Bruno smile with relief. And to her absolute joy, he got all his other lines right, too. The show was a triumph and all the people in the audience loved it.

Everyone, that is, apart from the caretaker, who often went round with a mean expression on his face. Anna-Lise overheard him telling one of the parents that he thought it was boring and what was the point of school plays anyway. Just more work for him, clearing up afterwards. The parent he was talking to was shocked to hear him say that, but he soon started giggling.

While the head teacher was telling everyone that they could go home, the caretaker's clothes began changing. Soon, instead of wearing a shirt and grubby jeans, he was wearing an old-fashioned nightgown, a floppy nightcap and a candle appeared in his hand. Suddenly, one of the men in the audience called out.

'Look!' he shouted. 'The caretaker's turning into Scrooge from *A Christmas Carol*!' Everyone began to laugh and point.

The children went to find their parents, who were all laughing uncontrollably. The head teacher was desperately trying to make herself heard over the noise of all the laughter. Bruno looked around the hall with a broad smile on his face. He knew exactly what had caused the transformation.

The caretaker was wondering why everyone had begun to laugh. He had not noticed the change in his appearance until he looked around and saw himself in a mirror. He let out a yelp and ran out, pulling his nightgown up so he would not trip up.

Anna-Lise was very pleased with herself. That was the most un-Christmassy person she had ever seen. She carefully climbed down the gym bars, and made her way through a sea of legs to where Bruno was standing with his mum.

'You were absolutely brilliant!' beamed Mrs Watson to Bruno as he put his coat on. 'That was the best school Christmas show so far!' Bruno glowed with pride. All that hard work rehearsing and learning lines had definitely been worth it.

'I loved that trick at the end with the caretaker's changing clothes. How on earth did he do that?' Bruno didn't know what to say. And then he felt something fall into his coat pocket.

That's weird, he thought to himself. When he put his hand into his pocket, he soon knew what it was that had fallen into his pocket. Or rather, *who* it was that had jumped into his pocket. While his mother was talking to another parent, he quickly whispered to Anna-Lise.

'I can't believe you made it!'

'It ok. It worth it to see your show. You was magtastical!'

'Thank you. I really enjoyed it. I couldn't have done it without your help, though.'

'Yes, you could,' she said. 'You just needed… guiding in right direction.'

On the way back from school, Bruno and his mother talked about the show and all of their favourite parts. Anna-Lise was straining to hear what they were saying. When they had nearly reached home she heard Mrs Watson say something to Bruno.

'As you were so brilliant, I'm going to tell you a secret.' She lowered her voice and said something to Bruno, but Anna-Lise could not make out what it was.

'That's brilliant! Thanks Mum!'

When they had got up to his bedroom, Bruno fished out Anna-Lise from his pocket.

'What is secret your mother say to you?' she asked.

Bruno looked solemnly at her. 'That, Anna-Lise, is a secret.'

'But Mr Bruno, you not have secrets from me! What she say?'

'I seem to remember a certain nisse telling me that it is a good thing to be patient. Well, now it's your turn to be patient. You will find out soon enough.'

Anna-Lise sighed. 'But that's not fair! I want to know now.'

'Patience, Anna-Lise, patience.' Bruno let out a little laugh when he saw just how bright purple Anna-Lise's face had become.

18th December
Prize Pudding

Anna-Lise was still wandering around frustrated. She did not like to be left in the dark. She decided to approach Bruno for the twelfth time that day.

'Please to tell little Anna-Lise your little secret. You such a nice boy, Mr Bruno. You want not upset Anna-Lise, do you?'

'If you think you're gonna get round me that easily, you're going to have to think again!' Bruno announced. He was amused by the situation. He had never seen Anna-Lise quite like this before.

'Ok, we change subject.' Anna-Lise had given up trying to find out... for now. 'What is the thing your mother is making now in kitchen?'

'I think she's making the Christmas pudding. It's weird. She's never done that before. We've always just bought one from a shop, but for some reason this year she's decided to make it herself.'

'I approve muchly,' she exclaimed. 'Home-made cakes is good. But what is this Christmas pudding?'

'You don't have Christmas pudding in Denmark?' asked Bruno, astonished.

'We have a pudding for Christmas, but it not look anything like what your mother making.'

'Well,' Bruno explained, 'it's in the shape of an upside down bowl. And there's loads of fruit in it. And nuts, I think. It's really rich.'

'It have much money? How can a pudding be rich? I not understand?'

'No, Anna-Lise, it's not a pudding that has lots of money, though there is some money inside the pudding. A coin – usually an old-fashioned sixpence.'

'Six pence is not much money! But I suppose maybe this is rich for a pudding. Puddings don't normally have money in, do they?' she asked.

'No, I don't think you quite understand. With food, rich means that it's very heavy. There also happens to be a coin in the pudding, but that's nothing to do with it being rich.'

'So why there a coin in pudding?'

'Dunno, it's just if you get the coin in your portion, you are the winner.'

'This excellent. What prize you win?'

'You don't win a prize. You win the honour of being the winner.'

'That very noble. In Denmark we also have same kind of thing. We have a rice pudding with many chopped almond nuts. But there is one almond nut that is whole, not chopped. And the person who gets the whole almond wins a prize – something little that is Christmassy like a chocolate or tree decoration or a book.'

'But what if you chew on the whole almond?'

'Now there is the secret of eating Danish Christmas rice pudding,' she explained. 'You must eat very carefully. For if you cannot show your whole almond, you cannot win a prize.'

'That's not fair! But I guess it just means everyone is really careful,' said Bruno.

'Absodefinitely they are careful.'

'And is that what they have in Australia, too?' Bruno had tried to get Anna-Lise to tell him about Australian Christmas almost since they had met. He thought he would give it another try.

'No, not in Australia. In Australia … but it getting late. I tell tomorrow.

And with a quiet

she disappeared.

19th December
Sydney

'Oki-doki. Pick me up, please, Mr Bruno.'

'What for?' asked Bruno.

'Just do it.'

Bruno put her carefully in his hands and Anna-Lise started to spell very carefully, 'S-Y-D-N-E-Y!'

Bruno felt a sudden jolt, and everything went black for a moment. Then he was blinded by a bright light and he began to feel very warm indeed. As the brightness faded he noticed that they were standing facing an enormous iron bridge with a strange white building on their left.

'This, Mr Bruno, is Sydney,' Anna-Lise explained.

'Wow! You mean Sydney in Australia? But that's on the other side of the world!'

'Yes indeedy,' the nisse said. 'You wanted to know about Australian Christmas, yes? Best way is to see it. It is, as you say, on completely the other side of world so everything is topsy-turvy, especially the weather. What you notice about the weather?'

'It's baking hot!' sighed Bruno, taking off his sweater.

'Yes! In Europe at Christmas time we have cold winter, but in Australia, it is the middle of summer and it very hot. But for many Australians, their families came from Europe, and they still have some traditions the same.'

'What's that noise?' asked Bruno.

'You listen carefully and tell me what you hear,' Anna-Lise suggested.

Bruno stood still and listened intently. He soon recognised the sound as singing. When he turned around, he saw he was in a big park and hundreds of people were singing *Deck the Halls*.

It felt strange to Bruno to hear such a Christmassy song in the summer heat with white parrots squawking in the trees. He looked up and saw black shapes flying in the sky. They looked like birds with very strange shaped wings.

'Anna-Lise, what are those black birds hovering over us?' he asked.

'They is not birds, Mr Bruno,' she replied.

Bruno looked closer, and it slowly dawned on him what they were.

'Bats! There are bats circling overhead and parrots all around us with people singing Christmas carols. That's weird!'

'It weird to you, maybe,' said Anna-Lise, 'but this totally normal here. Cockatoo parrots live everywhere here. Come, I show you more things. Take me this way.' She pointed the way to go.

Bruno went where Anna-Lise directed him and soon they were walking down a shopping street in the warm sunshine, surrounded by Christmas lights and shop windows with fake snow. They stopped at a large department store whose windows had moving nativity scenes. Only they were quite different from the ones in England. The baby Jesus, Mary, Joseph, the shepherds and kings were all represented by strange looking animals.

'Look, Mr Bruno,' said the nisse, 'there is a wombat, and three kangaroos as the wise men, an emu and some koalas. All Australian animals.'

'Wow!' said Bruno. 'It's all very Christmassy, but just in a very different way. What do they do on Christmas Day? Do they have the same food as us?'

'Some people do, but it usually very hot and sunny on Christmas Day,' Anna-Lise explained. 'Come, I show you. We go to seaside.' Anna-Lise closed her eyes and solemnly spelt out another word.

'B-O-N-D-I,' she whispered.

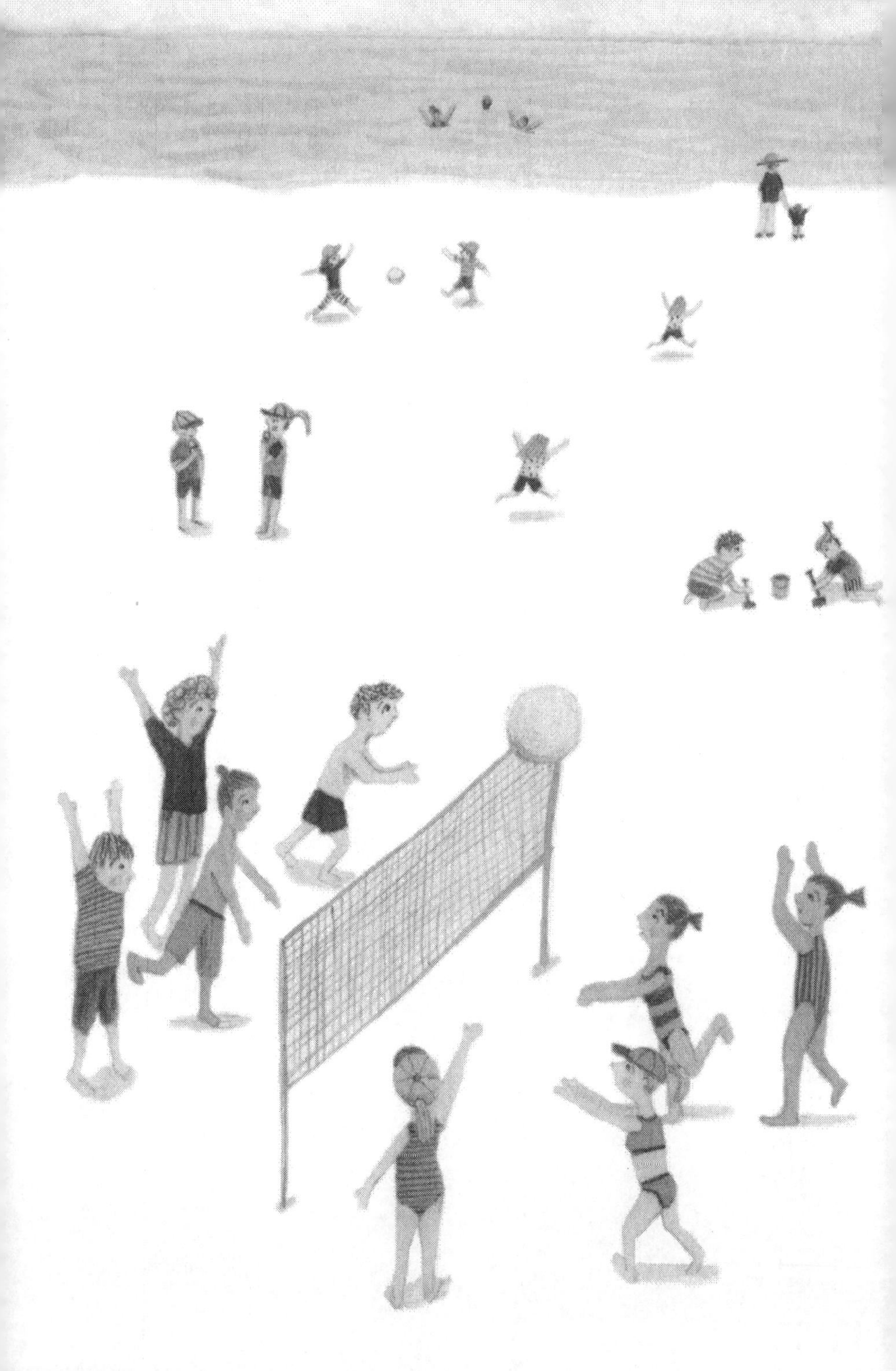

And in just a few seconds they had gone from the middle of a shopping street to the most enormous beach Bruno had ever seen.

'Tell me, Mr Bruno, what you see.'

'Well,' he began, 'there are loads of people on the beach. Some people swimming in the water and some surfers. And, look, there's a group of people playing cricket. And a family over there having a barbeque!'

'Good observing skills, Mr Bruno!' Anna-Lise was pleased. 'Many people in Australia have their favourite kind of dinner at Christmas – a barbeque! Imagine having a Christmas barbeque in England? It much too cold there, but over here it perfect weather for it. Everything you see here is things people like to do at Christmas.'

'What about Father Christmas delivering presents?' asked Bruno. 'If he's in Europe on Christmas Eve and Britain on Christmas Day when does he go to Australia? We must be thousands of miles from Britain!'

'Now this bit very clever,' explained Anna-Lise. 'Time is different here. I tell you things are topsy-turvy here. Well, when it is daytime in Europe it is night in Australia. So the Christmas Man, he deliver presents on afternoon of Christmas eve in Europe countries. Then gets a high-speed sleigh ride to the North of Australia.'

'Don't the reindeer get tired out if they have to go all round Australia as well?'

'They probably would if they did, but it is not reindeers who go round Australia. It much too hot for them here. They used to freezing conditions. They sweat too much if it very hot. They go into cool room in a city called Darwin and meanwhile the Christmas Man gets changed from his warm fur-lined boots into sandals and swaps his furry clothes for shorts and a colourful shirt.'

'So if he hasn't got the reindeer,' Bruno asked, 'then how does Santa get around Australia?'

'I think you can guess, Mr Bruno. What is most famous Australian animal?'

'They're kangaroos!' he called out. 'Of course!'

'Yes, they kangaroos with magic powers for one night a year. They take Father Christmas around Australia delivering presents. Then when they finish, they go back to Darwin, he change his clothes back and the reindeer are rested so they fly back to Britain and on to America. So it very busy few hours for the Christmas Man. Anyway, magic nearly running out. It time to go home. Close your eyes, Mr Bruno.'

Anna-Lise spelt out a few words quietly, and seconds later they were back in Bruno's bedroom.

'Wow, what an amazing adventure! Thanks, Anna-Lise! It's lucky Santa only does it once a year,' said Bruno. 'I reckon he needs the rest of the year to recover.'

'Oh, there is many worse jobs than being the Christmas Man. He loves it. By the way, what present you get for your mother this year?'

'Present? For Mum? I don't normally get her anything. I thought Father Christmas got for her.'

'Yes, this true, but it nice also for her to get something from *you*, yes? To say a thousand thank yous for all the things she does for you?'

'Yes!' agreed Bruno. 'Absodefinitely! What shall I get her?'

'This for you to decide, Mr Bruno, not me!'

'Well, I think we're going shopping tomorrow,' he said, 'so I could try to get something when she's not looking.'

'Or you make something yourself for her, maybe?' she suggested.

Bruno had a good think about what kind of thing his mum might want for Christmas. As he lay in bed, he had an idea.

'Anna-Lise,' he whispered. 'I know just what I'm going to get for Mum.'

20th December
Shopping

It was the last day of term, and Mrs Watson had told Bruno that they were going into town straight after school finished. He wanted Anna-Lise with him to help choose the right thing, but they were not going back home between school and town, so he'd had to bring her with him into school that day.

It had been very difficult keeping her hidden. She was curious to find out what was happening all the time, so she kept hopping out of his pocket, and he then had to try to find her without anyone noticing. One time, he finally found her inspecting some models of snowmen that his class had made.

'How many times do I have to tell you to stay in my pocket?' said Bruno.

'These good models but I disappointed. All snowmen – no snowgirls. S'no fair.' Bruno picked her up while no-one was looking and put her into his pocket.

'Now, please stay in my pocket!' And so she did. For another few minutes, anyway. But before long, the urge to explore became too much for her and, when Bruno wasn't looking, she hopped out and went to take a look at all the Christmas cards that were displayed in the classroom.

Bruno noticed she was gone, but gave up looking for her and trusted that she would do what was needed to stay secret. She didn't let him down. At the end of school, she came back to him and hopped back into his pocket without anybody seeing.

Bruno got into his mum's car and they drove into town. After going around several shops they finally got to a large department store. He wanted to show Anna-Lise what he was going to get for his mum, but Mrs Watson wouldn't let him out of her sight. It wasn't safe for Bruno to go around a shop by himself, but he also didn't want his mother to see what he was getting her.

'Psst. Psst, Bruno! I have an idea.'

Bruno waited for his chance to find out what it was. His mother was trying on a pair of shoes and he knelt down, pretending to do his shoelaces up.'

Intrigued, she agreed to the deal and dutifully kept her eyes closed the whole time, while Bruno found what he was looking for. Anna-Lise told him her plan and he approved. So once they left the shoe department, he made a deal with his mother. For five minutes, holding on to his hand all the time, she would have to keep her eyes shut as he led her around the shop.

He showed it to Anna-Lise and she approved very much of what he had chosen. He led his mother to the till where the shop assistant served Bruno, smiling

with amusement at the lady with the closed eyes. He used his pocket money to buy the present.

When it was all done, and the present was safely hidden in a bag, Bruno told his mother she could open her eyes again. Anna-Lise's plan had worked brilliantly. Bruno was safe all the time and Mrs Watson didn't have a clue what Bruno had got her. And she knew better than to ask him. She knew she had another few days yet to wait before she would find out. It was almost as difficult for Bruno. He knew his mother would really love it and he could hardly wait to see her face when she opened up her present.

21ˢᵗ December
The Shortest Day

The school holidays had just begun, so Bruno was really happy. December had been amazing, but now what he wanted more than anything was just for Christmas to be here. After a breakfast of warm porridge and maple syrup, he found some wrapping paper and he went to his room to find his mother's present. But when he went in, he found Anna-Lise sitting on the bookcase, crying.

'What's wrong Anna-Lise? Why are you upset?' he asked. Through her sobbing, she just about managed to make sense.

'It... it not good... day today,' she sniffed.

'Oh! Why is today not a good day?' Bruno asked.

'It 21st in December. It shortest day of the year,' the nisse explained. 'Not many hours of lightness today. Very short daytime. Very long night time.'

'What's so bad about that?' asked Bruno. He was confused. Why should this upset her so much?

'That not reason I crying.'

'So what is the reason?' Bruno asked.

'It means that I not many days have left here. Soon I must go back home and leave my English adventure. This make me feel many things. I sad because I have to go, but I happy because I see family again soon, but then I guilty because I feel happy and I not want you to be angry and think I happy to leave.'

'Don't be silly!' said Bruno. 'You've made this the best December I've ever had, Anna-Lise! Why would I ever be angry with you? You're always so much fun and you've been such a good friend to me. Ok, you've landed me in a few tricky situations, but what an adventure it's been! And it's not over yet, is it? There's still a couple of days left.'

'Yes, this true,' she admitted, 'but what we shall do in these days? I not have any ideas more.' She had stopped crying by now and blew her nose on her tiny handkerchief.

'Well, I think it's time *I* had some ideas for *you*, don't you? I know exactly what you need.'

'A mince pie?' she asked hopefully. 'With custard?'

'Nopi-dopi,' Bruno smiled. 'It's time you found out what the secret was from a few days ago. Remember, the one my Mum told me and that you wanted to know about?'

'But of course I remember. Yes, I want to know, I want to know muchly. Tell me please. I like to know secrets. I like always to know secrets.'

'The secret is...' said Bruno slowly.

'Yes? Please to tell. Please to tell!' Anna-Lise yelled excitedly.

'I will if you give me a chance.' It was good to see Anna-Lise in a cheerier mood again. 'Tomorrow evening...' Bruno paused to make it more dramatic.

'Yes?' Anna-Lise immediately put both hands over her mouth. She didn't want to interrupt but hadn't been able to help herself. By now she was jumping up and down with excitement.

'Tomorrow evening,' he repeated, 'we are going to the theatre to see the Pantomime.' Anna-Lise stopped jumping. Her mouth gaped wide open and she stared at Bruno with a small tear in her eye.

'You do this for Anna-Lise? You get tickets to thing I want most in whole world? You is lovely boy, Bruno. I think I never met nicer boy.'

'Well, to be honest it was Mum that got the tickets.'

'Yes, but it you who ask her for me,' she said.

'Not just for you. For me too. I wanna go to the panto too.' By now, Anna-Lise had fully recovered and was jumping up and down again.

'What is story? Is the one about the cat and the bells that tell him to be the Lord Mayor? Is the Aladdin lamp one?'

'Nopi-dopi. It's the best panto story there is: Cinderella!'

'Yippie-doodie!' Anna-Lise cried out. 'But this is my favouritest story of all time ever! Mr Bruno, a thousand, thousand thank yous! This means much to me,' and she gave his leg a big hug. And so that night, her dreams were full of pumpkins and ugly sisters and princes and castles.

22ⁿᵈ December
Pantomime

Anna-Lise woke up especially early. She knew it wasn't until the evening that they were going to see *Cinderella*, but she was very excited. She heard the door start to creak open and so with a well-practiced wave of her hand, a quick bit of spelling, and a faint *ping* she disappeared from view. Mrs Watson came into Bruno's room and woke him up with a gentle shake.

'Bruno, I need a sock,' she said.

'What? Oh, right. Yeah. Just a sec.' Bruno got up, opened a drawer and had a good rummage around. He pulled out one of his football socks.

'Yes, I thought that might be the one you would go for,' said Mrs Watson, 'the biggest one you've got! I'll just hang it up downstairs next to the fireplace.' She closed the door and Bruno went back under his duvet.

'Why wants your mother a smelly sock?' asked Anna-Lise as she made her way out from inside the cupboard.

'For my stocking. You know, my Christmas stocking,' explained Bruno.

'Ah, yes. You hang up and little presents in it waiting for you to open on Christmas morning. This fantasticous. A bit like they do in the Netherlands. They put a boot near the chimney and in the morning they get presents that have been thrown down chimney by person called Black Peter.

'Who's Black Peter? Anything to do with Blue Peter?'

'I not know who he is, really,' she said. 'But I think he work for Saint Nicholas.'

'Isn't that just another name for Santa?'

'You right, Bruno. Saint Nicholas was too long for people to say, so they then say Saint Nick, then just Santa. It keep getting shorter and shorter.'

The rest of the day went very slowly for Anna-Lise. She couldn't help thinking about the pantomime, she was looking forward to it so much. Finally, she heard Mrs Watson call up the stairs.

'Time to go, Bruno!'

Anna-Lise hopped into Bruno's pocket and off they went to the theatre. It all seemed very grand to the nisse. There was gold and red velvet everywhere and there were hundreds of people. The atmosphere was electric. People were going round with flashing wands and crowns on their heads. Their seats were in the Circle, which confused Anna-Lise very much. It meant that they were in the upstairs part of the theatre, but she didn't have a clue why upstairs was called a circle when it was more like a rectangle.

When the show started, Anna-Lise came out in goosebumps. She had a great view as they were in the front row. The performance was magical. She thought the girls in the show were very pretty (apart from the two ugly sisters).

'The ugly sisters are really being played by men,' Bruno whispered to her.

'They are? They very strange-looking men! You not tell me that Cinderella really a boy?'

'No, she is a girl. But the prince is also a girl.'

'But if prince is girl, then should be princess, not prince, yes?' By now Anna-Lise was quite confused, but loving every minute.

'It's a girl pretending to be a boy,' he explained. 'So the actress is playing the part of the prince.'

'Oh, I see! I love it. It much confuzzeling but it wonderific!'

After the show had finished, and Cinderella had seen off the ugly sisters to marry the prince, they made their way home. Bruno thanked his Mum for taking him to see it, but she said that she had enjoyed it lots too, and she was really pleased to see him joining in with all the audience participation.

As Bruno got into bed, Anna-Lise appeared at his feet with a *ping*

'Is excellent Christmas tradition,' she said with a smile. 'One of best!'

'Oh, no it isn't!' Bruno joked.

'Oh, yes it is, Mr Bruno!' she said. 'People there all having fun and laughing and it all make me so happy. Many thank yous, Mr Bruno! I write much about it.' She sat down at the end of the bed, opened her little furry book and began to scribble, writing down everything she had experienced that evening.

23rd December

Little Christmas Eve

Bruno walked into his room and saw Anna-Lise jumping up and down on his bed.

'Happy Little Christmas Eve!' she called to him.

'What's Little Christmas Eve?' he asked.

'Is the evening before Christmas Eve, of course,' she explained. 'Is the evening to spend time with family and play games and have fun and, of course, hygge!' Bruno looked sad.

'But I haven't really got a family to spend time with. It's alright for you. They'll all be waiting for you when you go back, but I've just got Mum, and she's usually too busy for fun.'

'Your mother is here tonight, yes?' Anna-Lise checked.

'I guess,' muttered Bruno.

'And she is in your family, yes?'

'S'pose so. But it's not the same as it used to be.'

'Oh, Mr Bruno. Of course not,' she said, 'things are never same as used to be. You is not alone. There many people who not have a mother or father around much of time. But only having one parent around does not mean you cannot have good time. You will have a wonderful evening, I promise! And you will have your mother all to yourself. This something special to treasure. Tonight is a night for hygge! You will play games!'

'What sort of games?' he asked. 'I don't think my Mum will want to play any computer games.'

'I not mean games on silly machines. I mean proper games. Board games. You ask your mother to look what games you have.'

So that evening, Bruno suggested to his mum that they play some games. She thought it was an excellent idea and opened up the games chest.

'Let's see what we have here.' Mrs Watson went through the chest, finding games she had not played for years. Then she stopped searching.

'What's this?' She took out a box that was wrapped in Christmas paper.

'Bruno, did you put this here?' she asked.

'No, it must have been a Christmas elf.' Bruno had decided to be completely truthful. He knew that his Mum would not believe him, so he was safe to say it.

'Really? Well, that's very kind of the elf.' She unwrapped the box and it was a game that she had never heard of, but she thought it looked fun. She read the rules out to Bruno. Every time you captured a piece on the board, you had to eat one of the chocolates. They both liked the idea of the game very much.

Before starting the game, Mrs Watson went to the kitchen to get herself a drink. She was quite surprised to find a mug on the table. It was filled with a spicy red liquid and had a label attached which said:

She smiled and heated it up. The spicy smells that came from the mug were wonderful. As she took a sip, she stopped suddenly, as distant memories flickered through her mind.

When she went back into the living room, she carried a bowl of peppernuts.

'Happy Little Christmas Eve, Bruno!' she said. Bruno wondered how she knew it was called Little Christmas Eve.

'Let the games begin!' Mrs Watson declared. Bruno and his mum had a wonderful evening. He was having such a good time playing the game, eating chocolate and munching peppernuts that he didn't even notice that Anna-Lise was missing. She was upstairs, slowly packing her bags.

24th December
Christmas Eve

Bruno was woken by a pounding on his stomach. He opened his eyes to see Anna-Lise jumping on him.

'Mr Bruno, Mr Bruno! Please to wake up! Please to wake up!' she called.

'I'm awake, don't worry, I'm awake,' said Bruno.

'Well, Mr Bruno, you know what today is. Is Christmas Eve and I must leave.'

'Do you really have to?' he pleaded. 'Couldn't you stay a bit longer?'

'You know I have to go. I must be back in time to be with my family tonight so I must set off now. Anyway, I think you not need me so much any more. I think you much happier boy than when I first meet you. You do many more fun things with your mother now. This much more important than me staying around.'

'I guess so. But it's been so great to have you here, Anna-Lise. Thank you for coming!'

'It my complete pleasure. Thank you for a wonderful December! I never forget it. I find out so many things and I think you learn things too,' she said with pride.

Bruno agreed. 'Defilutely!'

'Tell me, Mr Bruno,' she said, her face becoming more serious, 'you learn much about Christmas. But what you think is most important thing about Christmas?'

'I still think it's something to do with presents,' replied Bruno.

Anna-Lise looked a little worried.

'But I actually think the most important thing probably isn't to *get* presents. The thing I'm looking forward to most is to see Mum's face when she opens the luxury hot chocolate set I've got her.'

Anna-Lise's face beamed. 'Mr Bruno, you has made me much proud.'

'But it's not just about the presents, is it?' Bruno continued. 'I'm also looking forward to spending Christmas Day with Mum. We've had some really great days together these last few weeks. The best we've had for ages. It's something we can do all year round, but Christmas reminds us how important it is.'

'You is very clever and wonderific boy, Mr Bruno. I always remember you and I hope you do not forget completely about nisser. When it come to December month, please to remember me for as many years as you can. Even though you in England, I want you never to forget what we nisser stand for. Fun and happiness at Christmas. Hygge! And yummilicious food!'

'Of course I'll never forget you, Anna-Lise. You're one of the most amazing things that's ever happened to me. How could I *ever* forget you?'

'But what you do not realise, Mr Bruno, is that one day when you get older, you probably will forget. But that ok. This is the natural way of things with you humans. You grow older and most of you stop believing in things that do not make sense to you.

'But do not worry. One day, when you most need to remember about Christmas, a nisse will be sent to put the importance of Christmas back into your life. I have fantabulous time here with you. Many thank yous for teaching me about English Christmas. I tell all about it to my family.

'Farewell, Mr Bruno. I know we meet again sometime soon. Maybe next year you come to my home and have a Danish Christmas?'

Bruno's face lit up. 'That would be... briltastic!'

'Until next time, Mr Bruno.' Anna-Lise smiled, 'There just one more task for me to do before I go home.'

'What's that?' asked Bruno.

But Anna-Lise just beamed at him, closed her eyes and started to spell.

'D-I-S-A-P-P-E-A-R.' And with a quiet

she was gone.

Bruno stood still for a moment. He was sad that Anna-Lise had gone, but he was also looking forward to tomorrow. He fetched his mum's present, took it downstairs and placed it under the tree.

As Bruno went to sleep that evening, he heard a soft thud on the roof. He wanted to go out and look to see if it was who he thought it was, but he decided to stay in bed. He wanted to keep it a mystery. One of the things he had learnt from Anna-Lise was the importance of Magic. Some things are best left unexplained, he thought to himself.

Happier than he had been for a long time, he closed his eyes. He couldn't wait for tomorrow, but it did not take long for him to fall asleep. December had been amazing but also exhausting.

As he was drifting off, he thought he heard his mum's muffled voice in the corridor.

'Thank you, Anna-Lise. It's lovely to see a nisse again. There are so many things I'd forgotten, and not just about Christmas! Give my love to Erna.'

Bruno smiled as he imagined the look on his mum's face when she opened her present. He was looking forward to getting presents too, but somehow he didn't really mind what it was that he got.

Bruno fell into a deep, lovely sleep. His dreams that night were full of snowgirls, nisser and peppernuts. This was definitely Bruno's best Christmas ever.

Epilogue

On the other side of the street, Astrid Andersen peered out of the window. She watched as a familiar little light buzzed out of the house and darted up the street and out of sight.

She had kept an eye on the goings on in the house opposite, just as she had done many years ago when similarly strange things had happened. With a gentle smile she remembered the happiness she had felt as a young girl when a nisse came for a visit. She recalled how happy Mrs Watson had been all those years ago, when she had been a girl. In the past few weeks, that spark of life and happiness seemed to have returned to Mrs Watson.

Mrs Andersen looked forward to the next time a light came whizzing down the street. She didn't know when that would be, but she was certain of one thing. She would keep looking out of the window at midnight at the start of every December. Just in case.

As she drew the curtains and turned to finish making her rice pudding, she just caught a glimpse of a few flakes of snow fluttering down from the sky.

*Anna-Lise's Yumtastic Peppernuts Resipe

This mayks about 200 peppernuts. YUM!

Things you need to poot in:

220g plain flour
125g golden caster sugar
125g soft butter
½ teaspoon each of ground cinnamon, cardamon, cloves and allspice

1 egg
1 teaspoon baking powder
1 teaspoon vanilla extract

How to mayk them

1. Turn uven to 200°C.
2. Sieve all the dry things into a BIG bowl and mixty them into one big mess, until you have a quite solid dowe you can roll out.
3. Add the eggs and butter and vanilla and mix again
4. Roll into a few sausages about 1cm thick
5. Cut into 1cm cubies with a nighf or skissers.
6. Poot on bayking tray in batches. Kook in uven for about six minits until nearly brown. Mayk sure they are still a bit soft. Do not overcook!
7. Poot on cooling rake. Let them kool a bit.
8. Eat them all up in one go (if you is allowed!)

Made in the USA
Monee, IL
25 August 2019